First published in Great Britain in 2019 by Andersen Press Ltd.,
20 Vauxhall Bridge Road, London SW1V 2SA.
Text copyright © Sally Nicholls, 2019.
Illustration copyright © Bethan Woollvin, 2019.
The rights of Sally Nicholls and Bethan Woollvin to be
identified as the author and illustrator of this work
have been asserted by them in accordance with the
Copyright, Designs and Patents Act, 1988.
Printed and bound in China.
1 3 5 7 9 10 8 6 4 2
British Library Cataloguing in Publication Data available.
ISBN 978 178344 774 9

THE BUTTON BOOK

SALLY
NICHOLLS

BETHAN
WOOLLVIN

ANDERSEN PRESS

Here's a **red** button.
I wonder what happens
when you press it?

Here's an **orange** button.
What does the orange button do?

What happens when you
press the **blue** button?

It's a **singing** button!

"The wheels on the bus go round and round"

Does it know any other songs?

Shall we press
the **green** button now?

Thbbppppt!

Excuse me, say sorry
at once.

I'm warning you.
This is your last chance.

Thbbbpppt!

Well, if you're going to be like that,
we're going to press the **yellow** button instead.

Bounce!

It's a bouncing button!
Everybody bounce!

Bounce!

Bounce!

Bounce!

Bounce!

Help!

Press the **pink** button or
we'll be bouncing forever.

Hurrah, it's
a hug button.

Hug time!

That's the best
button of all.

You **do** want to press the next button?

Are you sure?

Are you really sure?

Please, press the **pink** button, **quick!**

"Hey— this is HUG time!"

HUG

Ahh...
that's better.
Hug time.

Oh no, it's that rude **green** button again.
Have you learned any manners yet?

Ah, the **blue** button.
What shall we sing this time?

"Twinkle, twinkle, little star..."

Back to the **red** button again.

Do you remember
what noise it makes?

Beep!

Look, it's a **new** button.

What does a **white** button do?

Shhhh... it's a sleeping button.

Goodnight, everyone.

zzzz

zzzzz